Translation copyright © 2005 by Christopher Franceschelli
All rights reserved · CIP data available
Published in the United States 2005 by Handprint Books
413 Sixth Avenue, Brooklyn, New York 11215
www.handprintbooks.com

First American Edition
Originally Published in Germany as Rosi in der Geisterbahn
© 2005 Beltz & Gelberg
in der Verlagsgruppe Beltz · Weinheim Basel

Printed in China
ISBN 1-59354-115-5 trade
ISBN 1-59354-130-9 library
2 4 6 8 10 9 7 5 3 1

Rosie
and the
Nightmares

Philip Waechter

HANDPRINT BOOKS BROOKLYN, NEW YORK

Rosie looked deep into the dark red maw.
Sharp teeth glittered. Rosie knew her hour had come.

She had only seconds left…

Rosie woke up. Her whole body was shaking and her fur was soaking wet.

 It had been like this for
weeks. Every night
those horrible dreams.

 It had to stop.

Rosie was sick and
tired of it.

 Time to get help.

So Rosie went to visit the
dream specialist.

"Hmmm, a clear case of fear of monsters. Hardly uncommon, but very unpleasant," said the dream specialist. "I'm going to write you a prescription for a wonderful book. Read it thoroughly, practice all the exercises, and you'll soon be back in the pink of health."

Rosie didn't waste a minute. She rushed to the bookstore and bought the book the good doctor had recommended.

It was a great book. All day and all night she pored through it. Soon she had learned how to deal with monsters.

She learned how to be a calming
influence upon them…

…how to incapacitate a monster
with a simple throw…

…and how to take to her heels in
an emergency.

With her newfound knowledge,
Rosie hatched a plan.

She was ready to put her plan into action.

Rosie jumped into a cab.

"Please take me there as fast as you can," she told the driver. "I have something very important to do and can't afford losing even a moment."

Soon she found herself standing in a long line. Step by step she reviewed her plan. Nothing could go wrong.

Finally it was Rosie's turn. She bought a ticket at the window.

She buckled herself into the most beautiful
car, handed her ticket to the man with the
checkered cap, and drove off.

Rosie's eyes adjusted quickly to the darkness. Everything was just as creepy as she had imagined. Huge eyes stared at her. Pointy teeth flashed.

Sharp claws scratched. Great mouths hissed. Rosie took one last deep breath. There was no turning back now. She was ready.

Rosie jumped out of her car.

With a few clever moves...

...she dispatched the first monster. Then another. And another.

For the biggest and most gruesome she had
planned something especially mean.

The beasts stampeded away, screeching. This was starting to be fun. But nothing lasts forever.

"Could someone please tell me what's going on here?" the man with the checkered cap shouted. "Enough. Stop. Everybody back to your places. And you, Rabbit, you're coming with me!"

"I never want to lay eyes on you again," the man scolded. "Just like a rabbit, nothing but mischief on the brain."

Rosie, however, cheerfully set off for home.

Rosie decided that she deserved a treat. Three scoops of ice cream. To top it all off, she celebrated with a cup of Jasmine tea.

After dinner, Rosie settled down to read a chapter in her book. But as it turned out, she had something better to do...